PONY CAMP diaries

Sophie and Shine

by Kelly McKain

Illustrated by Mandy Stanley

Stripes

To Rob,
and Janet Rising for all the
invaluable pony advice.

THIS DIARY BELONGS TO

Sophie

Dear Riders,

A warm welcome to Sunnyside Stables!

Sunnyside is our home and for the next week it will be yours too! We're a big family – my husband Johnny and I have two children, Millie and James, plus two dogs ... and all the ponies, of course!

We have friendly yard staff and a very talented instructor, Sally, to help you get the most out of your week. If you have any worries or questions about anything at all, just ask. We're here to help, and we want your holiday to be as enjoyable as possible – so don't be shy!

As you know, you will have a pony to look after as your own for the week. Your pony can't wait to meet you and start having fun! During your stay, you'll be caring for your pony, improving your riding, enjoying long country hacks, learning new skills and making friends.

And this week's special activity is a day out riding in a beautiful horse-drawn carriage! Add swimming, games, films, barbecues and a gymkhana and you're in for a fun-filled holiday to remember!

This special Pony Camp Diary is for you to fill with all your holiday memories. We hope you'll write all about your adventures here at Sunnyside Stables – because we know you're going to have lots!

Wishing you a wonderful time with us!

Jody xx

Monday afternoon
—I'm at Pony Camp!

We've just had lunch on my very first day at
Pony Camp, and I thought I'd start writing in
my fab new diary straight away. Jody, who runs
Sunnyside Stables, gave us one each to write
all our adventures in while we're here and I've
had such an exciting time already! We had our
assessment lesson this morning and I've been
given the best pony ever. She's called Shine and
she's absolutely gorgeous! I'll write more about
her in a minute but I'm going to start right at
the beginning so I don't miss anything out.

We were a bit late arriving because my
baby brother Albie was screaming and Dad
couldn't get him strapped into the car seat.
Plus, Mum had to pack all his stuff, like his
bottles and nappies and pushchair, and
even with me helping it took ages.

Albie needs as much for one car journey as I do for a week!

So by the time we got here everyone else was already unpacked and on the yard. Jody showed me upstairs and I had to quickly dump my stuff in the room where I'm staying. I took the top bunk, as someone's towel and nightie were already on the bottom one. There was also an unmade bed by the window covered in soft toy ponies, and Jody told me it belonged to her daughter, Millie.

Jody   Millie   Sally

I hurried down to the yard and Sally the head instructor gave us a welcome talk, and introduced all the yard staff. Then Jody told us

about bedtimes and meals and stuff, and said
to come to her if we had any problems or
questions. Jody's really nice and though she's
Millie's actual mum, she's going to be like a mum
to all of us while we're staying here.

Then Sally got us to introduce ourselves to
each other and I found out that
the other girl (on the bunk below
me) is called Beth. She's my age but
a bit smaller than me, and she's got
lovely wavy hair (I'm always trying to
get mine to go like that but it never
does!). She looked a bit nervous and
asked me if I'd done much riding before.

Beth

I explained that while I've been riding for
quite a few years, I don't get to go very often
any more because of Mum and Dad being so
busy with Albie. "So I've done lots of flatwork
and some jumping but I've probably forgotten
loads of it," I told her. "Actually, that's one of

the things I'm most looking forward to on this holiday – working on my riding non-stop for a whole week!" Then I suddenly panicked, thinking what if Millie and Beth are really good, but Beth said, "I've done way less than you – I only started a few months ago, when me and Dad moved down here."

We both turned to Millie at the exact same time and said, "I bet you're brilliant," which was so spooky it made all three of us collapse into giggles. Millie said, "I've been riding a long time, but if I can get my pony to do what I want it's a miracle." Her pony's called Tally and she says his main hobby is bombing off on hacks and dragging her through hedges.

Sophie and Shine

The other girls are lovely too, and I especially like Shanice. She's really smiley and said she liked my new black cord jodhs (I had to get new ones because when I tried on my riding stuff last week I'd grown out of my old ones!). Shanice lives in London and she's hardly ridden at all, but she's so pony mad she saved up for a really nice grooming kit to use on her pony this week. She got given a cute piebald called Prince and she fell in love with him straight away.

The three older girls are really cool. Aneela has amazingly long shiny hair and Izzy's got a fab purple silk she bought specially for this week. Courtney's wearing make-up and when I said I liked her eyeshadow she offered to do a makeover on me one night! Her mum's actually a beauty therapist so Courtney's learnt all about

make-up and hair and face packs and stuff
from her. Who haven't I mentioned yet? Oh,
yes, Daisy and Grace are the youngest, they're

identical twins and even their
riding gear is exactly the same (I
don't know how we'll ever tell
them apart!).

After a quick tour round
the yard, we were all given
our ponies. It was so exciting
waiting to hear who I'd got. Sally
read our names off a list as Lydia brought the
ponies out one by one, and that's when I met
my gorgeous Shine!

Lydia had tacked up the ponies for us this
once but we'll be doing that ourselves for the
rest of the week. It's so great that we get to do
everything for them as well as all the riding. It's
almost like actually owning one. I used to ask
and ask and ask Mum and Dad if I could have

my own pony, but they kept saying no, so I
stopped eventually. But it's still my number one
dream and I secretly think about it a lot and
imagine what it would be like.

Shine's exactly the sort of pony I've been
dreaming about! She's a really pretty bay
and so sweet and friendly. At 13.2hh
she's the perfect size for me too!
She's got a beautiful glossy coat
and I'm going to make it
gleam for the gymkhana
on Friday. I feel so lucky
that I got her!

I've brought my digital
camera and I've taken pix
of everyone and their ponies,
but there's nowhere here to print
them off, so instead I'll have to do
some drawings of us all. I know – I'll make it
into a puzzle.

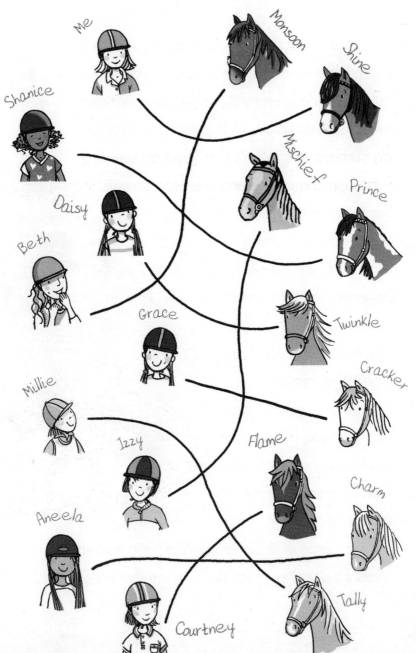

◡ Sophie and Shine ◡

As we were given our ponies, we led them over to the mounting block and got on, ready for the assessment lesson. I had to walk Shine away from the crowd a bit before sorting out my stirrups. She wasn't that keen on standing right near the others and she kept on swishing her tail and shifting about.

It felt strange being back on a pony at first, but in the assessment lesson we had a good long walk round on each rein, so I had time to think about my position and get used to Shine. We did lots of halts, circles and changes of direction to get our ponies listening to us. It took me a while to remember to look around to see where I was going, though! Shine is quite forward-going in trot so I could go rising in a nice rhythm without nagging her all the time. Sally called out to me to change my trot diagonal, though, and I realized I'd forgotten to even check it!

When we had a canter I slid my outside leg back and Shine did as I asked straight away. I'd forgotten how fast it felt – but also how fun! Sally had to tell me to sit back and down, and stop clinging to the reins, but I didn't really mind her saying that because she calls things out to everyone. Shanice hasn't cantered before so she had a trot instead, and Sally said she'd be cantering by the end of the week, no worries. It's great that things are coming back to me already – and it helps that Shine's so lovely to ride! It was just so exciting – and to think, I've got loads more canters to go before the end of the week!

Afterwards we untacked (I helped Shanice with Prince as she hadn't done it before), and then we all gathered back on the yard to hear what groups we'd be in. Sally said I was borderline but she's putting me in Group A to start off with (the beginners' group) so I can find my feet and brush up my skills. If I do well she's going to move me up to Group B. I'm really disappointed to be honest, and can't help thinking that if Mum and Dad hadn't been so busy with Albie. . . Still, I suppose moving groups can be a goal for me to work towards.

We then had a lecture about safety on the yard, and Lydia showed us where everything was and how to put things away properly so nothing got tripped over or lost. It was fun because she pretended to do dangerous things like mounting without her chin strap done up, or tying up a pony without using a slip-knot, and we had to stop her by calling out "No!" and saying what was wrong.

Then at lunch Aneela was doing impressions

of a teacher at her riding school at home who has this really snooty voice and we were all in stitches. She's so funny – in fact, all the girls here are nice. We've just been trying on each others' stuff. Daisy's blue fleece really suited Shanice and Izzy's purple silk looked great on Courtney's hat, and she said she really wishes she'd bought a new one before she came too. Grace insisted on trying on Aneela's jodhs and of course they were miles too long for her! I know I'm going to have a fab week with them all!

COURTNEY wearing IZZY'S silk

Jody just gave us our welcome letters (I've stuck mine in the front of this diary) and we found out we're going carriage-driving this week – we're all really excited. It'll be great fun going on a trip together and only Izzy has been in a carriage before, when she was a bridesmaid at her cousin's wedding, so it'll be a brand new horsey experience too!

We've got to go back on the yard again
now for our first Pony Care lecture – it's on
tack and tacking up. I'm going to pay extra
special attention in the lectures because maybe
if I show Mum and Dad how much I've learnt
they'll understand how serious I am about
getting my own pony, and then they might start
to think about it at least.

Monday, after dinner

Our lecture was really interesting – we learnt
about all the different bits of tack, then watched
Lydia demonstrate tacking up on Aneela's pony,
Charm. She chose him because he's so good
at standing still on the yard. Everyone laughed
when Millie said that if we'd used Tally it would
have been more like a demonstration of chasing
an escaping pony down the lane!

Then we had our first go at tacking up our
ponies. Millie has done all this before, so went
around helping the younger girls. We did it in
their stables and pens to make it easier, and we
worked in twos so we could help each other.
I went with Beth and she was really good
about helping me get the bit in (I've only done
it once before and I didn't want to bang poor
Shine's teeth with it). When I helped her with
Monsoon we played this game pretending they

were our own ponies and we were getting
ready for a big comp, and it was really cool.
Both is so much fun! When Lydia came round
and checked what we'd done all she had to do
was move Shine's girth up a hole, so we were
really happy!

Our lesson this afternoon was fun too.
Jody wanted us to just relax and get to know
our ponies, so we did lots of transitions and
changes of rein to get good control and then
we practised weaving in and out of cones. It
was so funny when Cracker decided he couldn't
be bothered to go round all the cones and just

carted Grace off to the end of the manège instead!

I also found out that Shine gets spooked easily! It was really windy this afternoon and during the lesson a shed door banged and sent her skittering off across the manège. It really freaked me out and my heart went all fluttery, but I managed to keep going and put her straight. But then she kept refusing to walk past the bit of fence where it happened and Jody said I had to ride really positively so Shine didn't go completely silly about it. I felt really nervous but I made myself act calm and after a while Shine was fine again. Jody called out, "You may not have ridden for a while, Sophie, but you obviously have a feel for ponies. You handled that very well!"

At this rate, maybe I really will get moved up

to Group B sometime this week! When we had
a canter, Shanice decided to trot again instead
and Jody gave her a big smile and said maybe
she can have another go tomorrow.

Oh, I nearly forgot. Something strange
happened before, when we were doing yard
duties. We all put our hard hats on the bench
in the tack room so we didn't have to take
them upstairs, and I volunteered to sweep the
main yard so I could look at Shine, because her
stable is right there. When the jobs were done
and Sally said it was time to go in for dinner,
we all went to pick up our hats. On the way in
to the farmhouse, Izzy was asking everyone if
they'd seen her silk (the really nice purple one),
because it's vanished. It was on her hat when
she left it in the tack room but when she went
back after yard duties, her hat was just black,
and the silk was nowhere to be seen. Millie
said not to worry, and that it probably got lost

behind something, and she's sure it'll turn up. But I think it's strange. I mean, how could Izzy's silk have come off the hat on its own?

Weird!

I like mysteries, so I am thinking of ideas about what could have happened. Like, maybe a girth strap caught on the silk while someone was putting their saddle away and pulled it off (not very likely, I know, but it's the best I can think of so far!).

Anyway, I have to go now because we're going swimming for our evening activity (there's a pool here – Millie is just so lucky!).

Monday night, in bed—
I'm quickly writing this by the light of my torch

Swimming was really fun – Millie's dad Johnny organized some water races and games, and then we had time to just play around. Me, Millie and Beth pretended to be synchronized swimmers and made up this whole routine (and completely got the giggles too!).

Afterwards, when we'd had our showers and dried off, we all had hot chocolate together in the kitchen. This really is turning out to be the perfect holiday!

Millie and Beth and me have all been whispering for the last hour, till they both fell asleep. Beth was telling us how her mum still lives in Manchester and how she hardly ever gets to see her. She's got no brothers and sisters, so it's just her and her dad. She says it's fine and she doesn't mind, but I felt really sorry for her – I can't imagine not having Mum around, even if she does spend most of her time with Albie at the moment. Thinking of not having Mum around all the time has made me start missing her, so I'm going to turn off my torch and try to get some sleep before I get really homesick! Goodnight!

Tuesday, we just had lunch, and I want to quickly write about my fab morning!

I had such a great time with Shine this morning, and Jody's lesson was really fun. She's even nice when she's telling you how to correct something. Like, this morning, I wasn't sitting back and down enough in my canter, and she called out, "Sophie, if you keep leaning on the reins I'll make you do it without them!" and everyone laughed.

Sally's group rides in the next manège and she quite often yells at them, not in a nasty way or anything but just kind of shouting, "Inside leg on!" so it's a bit more strict than in our group. I'm still hoping to move up this week, though!

Oh, and Shanice cantered this morning! She held the pommel the first time to get her confidence and then she had another go with just the reins. She was grinning all over her face when Prince came to a stop, and she gave him a big pat to say well done.

It was brilliant at the end of the lesson too, because Jody had us doing round-the-worlds as fast as we could – Beth was great at it, and we were all amazed by her whizzing legs, especially as she's only been riding a few months! But she said she used to be in the gymnastics team at her old school, so that explains it! Then we did riding with our arms out to the sides (as in with no reins) to help with our balance. Cracker kept wandering off across the manège, even though Grace was really using her legs, and that had us all giggling.

After our break, we went to the barn for a lecture. It was all about grooming and Daisy brought out some ribbons she'd bought specially to put in Twinkle's tail for the gymkhana (there's

a tack and turnout comp as well as the races
and stuff). She asked Lydia to show us how to
do a tail plait as well as a full groom, so we all
got to see how it was done.

The ribbons looked very smart tied on the
end of the plait and Lydia did
it really, really neatly, so now
we all want our ponies to look
like that for the gymkhana! She
borrowed Shanice's lovely brushes
for the grooming demonstration and then
when we did our own ponies, everyone was
asking if they could borrow them too. I brought
Shine into the barn to be with the other ponies
(most of them are turned out at night), and
after we'd given them a thorough groom we
had a go at the tail plaiting. It was much, much
harder than it looked and mine came out a bit
wrong, but Courtney helped me to sort it out.
She was really good at it and her fingers were

flicking over and under, and the plait got longer and longer at lightning speed. I even had to get her to slow down so I could see what she was doing. She said that her mum does French plaits for weddings and they're not all that different to tail plaits for ponies! There's still plenty of time for me to practise before Friday, luckily!

Tuesday, it's our free time after dinner (we had sausages and mash!)

Yum!

Oh dear, another strange thing has happened and now I don't know what to think. Millie and Beth are on washing-up duty at the moment (I'm on tomorrow with Shanice), so I've got a bit of time to write about it in my diary.

But first, let me just write about the fab pony stuff we did this afternoon. To start with, we had a lecture about road safety and first aid, and what to do if you get lost on a hack (which is find a landmark if possible and then call the yard for help), and then we actually went out on one all together! Me, Millie and

Beth chattered all the way round, apart from when we had to concentrate on trotting up the hills and going through this river without coming off and getting very wet! I really wish Millie and Beth lived near me so we could hang around together all the time. And I wish Shine could be my pony forever!

Then, when we got back, the strange thing happened. After the hack, we were untacking and doing yard duties, and when I went to put Shine's bridle back in the tack room, I found Daisy searching through her tack box with Grace and Shanice. They explained that

Twinkle's ribbons had gone missing. Daisy
looked a bit upset so I gave her a hug and said,
"Don't worry, we'll find them."

While they searched all over the tack room
and the yard, I went back to the barn where
we'd had the demonstration, in case the ribbons
had fallen into the straw. As I stood there, I
remembered something that hadn't seemed at
all important this morning. I'd noticed that while
we were packing away, Daisy's ribbons *did* fall
into the straw. I was about to go and get them
for her when Courtney picked them up. I turned
to get my hoof pick from Grace and of course
I just assumed that Courtney put them back in
Daisy's tack box – but what if she hadn't? They
certainly aren't there now. What if Courtney
thought no one was looking and sneaked them
into her pocket instead? Oh, that can't be true,
can it?

Suddenly I found myself thinking about Izzy's

purple silk as well, which still hasn't turned up.
Courtney was the one who tried it on her hat
when we were swapping stuff yesterday. But
surely she couldn't have taken it – and Daisy's
ribbons. Could she?

When I got back to the tack room the

ribbons still hadn't been
found, though.

"Listen, don't worry,
Mum's got a big box of
ribbons for everyone to use
for the gymkhana," Millie
was telling Daisy. "If yours
don't turn up, you can choose some new ones
from there. We'll let you have first pick, won't
we, girls?" We all nodded and Daisy cheered up
a bit after that.

Millie seems convinced that Daisy's ribbons
just got lost somewhere, but I'm not so sure.

After dinner just now, when we were all

clearing the plates away, I got up the courage to
ask Courtney if she'd seen Daisy's ribbons in the
barn at the end of the lecture. She didn't even
look startled or anything and she just said, "Yeah,
I did. They'd fallen into the straw so I just picked
them up and put them back in her tack box. They
must have gone missing after that." I was silent
for a moment, thinking, and she gave me a funny
look and said, "Why do you ask?"

I quickly shook my head and mumbled, "No
reason."

Luckily I can stop thinking about it now
because it's time to go outside. We were going
to have a film tonight because of the rain but it's
stopped now, so we're playing rounders instead.
I hope my team wins!

Still Tuesday, just!

Millie and Beth are asleep, but I feel wide awake after what just happened. I'm worried Millie thinks I'm a bit horrible or something. I wasn't going to say anything, but we had such a good time playing rounders together (we didn't win, but never mind!) and then whispering after lights out, that it just sort of came out.

First, I made them promise not to tell anyone and then I told them about how I'd seen Courtney pick up the ribbons in the barn, but that I wasn't sure if she really had put them into Daisy's tack box. And I reminded them that Courtney was the one who'd really liked the purple silk too.

They were both silent for a long time and I started to wish I hadn't said anything. Then Millie said, "But Sophie, we were all admiring Izzy's silk in the yard, and Courtney did say she'd put the ribbons back when you asked her."

"Yeah, I suppose so," I mumbled. "Beth? What do you think?" I whispered, but there was no reply. What a shame she'd fallen asleep just when I needed her to back me up.

Millie sighed loudly. "Look, the silk could have been pulled off Izzy's hat by accident and fallen down somewhere," she whispered. "And as for Daisy's ribbons, they could have blown out of her tack box as she came back across the yard, and maybe even been swept up by now. You can't just accuse someone – you have to be sure."

I didn't say anything after that. I just lay here, feeling really awkward. After a while Millie fell asleep so I found my torch and got out my diary. Oh, I really hope she doesn't think badly of me for mentioning it. And I'm glad Beth didn't hear me after all. Us three get on so well, it would be awful if we fell out over this!

I feel a bit better now I've written all that down. I'm going to try to sleep, so that the morning comes quicker and I can see Shine again. Jody says we're off on our carriage-driving trip tomorrow too – I'm really looking forward to that!

It's our free time
after lunch on Wednesday

I wolfed down my breakfast this morning so I
could be first out for yard duty. I couldn't wait
to see Shine and have a private talk to her
about what happened last night. After filling a
few of the water buckets for Lydia, I got on with
giving Shine a good groom before tacking up. As
I combed her mane, I told her all about the silk
and the ribbons in a low voice. I was careful
that no one overheard, especially because
by then the yard was busy with
all the girls getting their
ponies ready. Everyone
was talking about our
carriage-driving trip
— they were all just as
excited as me!

When I'd told Shine everything, she nuzzled into my shoulder, like she was telling me I was right to say something last night after all.

And it turns out I really was – because just then Shanice came running out of the tack room and straight over to Shine's stable. "Sophie, my body brush, from my grooming kit, it's disappeared!" she wailed, tears in her eyes.

"Are you sure?" I asked. She nodded miserably. "I cleaned my kit and put it away before dinner yesterday," she mumbled. "I even double checked I had everything because I'd been lending things out."

I came out of Shine's stable and put my arm round her. Millie, Daisy, Grace and Beth hurried over to find out what was wrong (the older girls were busy helping Lydia in the top barn).

As Shanice explained, I gave Millie a meaningful
look. She frowned and said, "Okay, it does look
like something funny is going on. Let's go to
Mum."

So we all marched off to the kitchen and told
Jody about the brush. We also mentioned the
silk not turning up, and about Daisy's ribbons
going missing. I felt so sorry for Shanice and I
really wanted to tell Jody what I suspected about
Courtney too, but Millie gave me a sharp look
and mouthed the words "no proof". She's right,
there isn't any, so I'll just have to find a way to
get some. I really think Courtney is stealing things
now and I can't let her get away with it.

I felt loads better when Jody took charge.
She sent Millie to ask the yard staff if anyone
had borrowed the brush in the evening without
putting it back (they hadn't). And she asked Beth
to go up to the top barn to bring back the older
girls, and then got us to check all the Sunnyside

tack boxes in case it had somehow been put back in the wrong one. We also looked in every stable, the office, the barns and the house.

When none of the things were found, Jody just stood frowning for a moment, thinking. Then she snapped out of it. "Right, girls, I'm sure we'll sort this out," she said briskly. "On a brighter note, Sophie, you're moving into Group B this morning. Well done for improving so much."

I couldn't believe it! I've done it! I've been moved up!

Everyone gave me a clap, which was so cool, and I couldn't help beaming. Then we had to hurry up and finish tacking up for our lessons, because we were running a bit late after hunting for the brush.

My first lesson in Group B didn't go that well, actually. I was a bit nervous that I wouldn't be able to do what the others could, and about letting Sally down, and I think Shine picked up on that. She was really skittish and, after she knocked down a pole on the jump we were popping, she kept spooking and running out at the last minute. Sally told me to try again and again, so Shine wouldn't think that being cheeky was going to get her out of jumping. I didn't really want to because I felt like it wasn't Shine's fault she didn't want to pop the jump, and that she was honestly scared. I wouldn't even give her an extra squeeze with my legs before going over, as Sally had asked me to.

Instead, I just kept failing, and I got more and
more flustered until Sally told me to come into
the middle and take a break. I did have another
go and I got Shine over in the
end, but I felt so annoyed with
myself. Sally must think I'm
a rubbish rider!

ME getting
FLUSTERED

At least it wasn't as if
everyone in Group B was
riding perfectly (which
is what I'd imagined!).
When we did some sitting
trot, Izzy lost her hold on
the reins and Mischief took
advantage, cutting the corner off, and Aneela
was bobbling around clutching Charm's mane.
Courtney called out, "Ow, my bum!" and
everyone else laughed, but I didn't feel like
joining in – I couldn't stop thinking about what
she'd done.

◡ Sophie and Shine ◡

Anyway, after a while in sitting trot I remembered to let my legs and seat bones go soft. Once I'd stopped trying to grip on, I got into a good rhythm and it was like my bum was glued to the seat — for a few strides anyway! I was hoping Sally would notice and she did, saying, "Well done, Sophie, lovely!" I'm glad she's seen me do one thing well. I can't wait to show Mum and Dad how much I've improved this week!

And the lecture was the best one we've had yet! It was called 'All About Ponies' and covered everything from points of the horse to colour and markings, conformation and breeds. I acted silly to make Shanice laugh and help take her mind off the missing brush.

Lydia obviously had the same idea as me about cheering Shanice up because she asked her to get Prince out of the barn to be the demonstration pony, and let her hold him while she showed us the points of the horse.

Aneela was really sweet to Shanice as well,
and she lent her this cool pink and purple
stripey lead rope to bring Prince out with. I'm
determined to catch the thief (you know who!)
and get Shanice her brush back, but I don't
know how. I'll have to try and come up with
a plan!

Anyway, after the demonstration bit, it was
really fun because we went round the yard in
twos seeing how many markings we could spot.
Me and Shanice spent ages trying to work out

whether Shine has a big snip or a short stripe!
In the end we decided that she's so special and
unique that maybe there isn't even a name for
her marking, so we made one up – a strinip!

I have to stop writing, as we're off on our trip
now. I've never been in a carriage before and I
can't wait! I wonder if it will be a grand one
like they sometimes have in those
old-fashioned shows on TV,
or more like a farm cart,
or even a racing chariot!
I wonder what the horses and
ponies will be like and if we'll
get to help put the harnesses and
stuff on them. I wonder … oh, I guess
I'll just have to wait and see!

"strinip"

Wednesday at 4.30pm

We're in the minibus on our way back from the carriage driving. Lydia says I'll make myself feel sick, writing on the move, but I don't want to forget anything about the trip because it was brilliant!

It took about half an hour to get to the farmhouse (Johnny drove us, and Lydia came too). When we got there, we met Fred and his wife, Marjorie, who are total carriage-driving fanatics. They took us round the barns, and showed us all their different coaches and traps and things. Some were really shiny and perfect and some were all in bits (Fred's hobby is restoring them). When he pointed out the trap we'd be riding in – a two-wheeler that only fitted one person

and the driver, we got even more excited.
Marjorie explained that we couldn't drive it
ourselves because it's not a skill you can just
learn in half an hour, but if we were lucky she
might give us a little go of the steering. So we
practised with these reins that were attached to
the wall in the barn. It's really different to normal
riding because you put both reins in your left
hand and just use your right as a guide.

We were all laughing because, well, for a
start we were driving a wall, and also, when we
got it wrong Marjorie was making up pretend
things that would happen if we really did steer
like that, saying, "Your horse would be in the
ditch right now," or "You'd have hit a tree by
the side of the road!"

Then we walked over to the stables and
everyone went really crazy over the horses and
ponies. There was a pair of greys a bit like Jody's
mare, Bonny, which pull carriages as a team, and

a pair of black horses that Fred called Hackneys – a breed that's really good at trotting. Then we met the pony who we were going to be driving – a gorgeous cobby gelding called Bayleaf – and everyone went even more crazy over him.

There are loads of different straps and things on a driving harness and Marjorie said it all has to go on in the right order or it's unlucky. There's a saddle, just like in normal riding, but it looks really different, like this:

Carriage
Saddle

NOT FOR
SITTING ON!

Also, the pony wears blinkers to stop him from looking behind at the carriage and you have to be really careful to make sure the blinkers fit properly. If they don't, they could rub

on the pony's eyes, or gape so that he can see
behind him after all and get scared by the trap.

When Bayleaf was all ready, Fred held him
while Marjorie attached the trap, and then we
all had a turn of sitting up in the carriage with
her. It was so brilliant trotting up and down the
lane, and Marjorie let me have a little go at the
steering too! It's weird because you can't use
your legs and seat (obviously!) but only your
hands and voice (they do use a whip sometimes
but I couldn't manage that as well!). It's amazing
to think that in the old days most transport was
actually horse-drawn, so you would have ridden
in a carriage or a trap everyday. Mum would
have had to let me get my own pony then. It
would have been just as normal as having a car!

I couldn't get the hang of the steering at first
and Bayleaf went a bit slow and wobbly, but I
soon got him going again. It was such a great
feeling rattling along the lane with the sound

of his hooves clip-clopping and the wheels clattering. Then Marjorie took over the steering and she got Bayleaf going so fast the carriage was really bouncing along. It was way better than the best fairground ride and I just couldn't stop grinning.

When we'd all had a go in the trap, we had a drink and some of Marjorie's home-made apple cake – yum! Then Fred took us to see one special coach he was restoring, which was in a barn on its own. It was really grand and a few of us could sit in it at once. I pretended to be in a film where they wear all the old-style costumes, like in Victorian times. Then the other girls joined in, and Lydia acted the part of our governess and really made us laugh by inspecting our fingernails and everything.

Oh, hang on, I do feel a bit sick actually – I'd better stop writing for now!

Wednesday at 8.16 pm

I ♥ this HOLIDAY!

We've just been swimming again and everyone's
milling around getting showered and dressed.
I'm just waiting for Millie and Beth to leave the
room so I can sneak out unnoticed. I've got a
fab plan to catch you-know-who in the act of
taking something else and I'm going to put it
into action.

I thought of it when we got back to the yard
this afternoon. We had some time with our
ponies, mucking out the stables and barn and
topping up their water and everything. I was
just telling Shine how I needed a plan to catch
the thief when something happened to give me
the answer.

I was about to take my barrow to the muck

heap when Lydia came along. She nudged the
bolt over on the bottom of Shine's door with
her foot. "Don't forget the kick bolt, Sophie,"
she said, smiling. "Some of the ponies have
a habit of sneaking out! In fact, one morning
there was so much hay missing we had to set
up a watch in the office overnight to find the
culprits."

I laughed and asked who they were.

"Cracker and Mischief," she said. "As I'd
guessed. They're out in the field
now, of course, but over
the winter we really have
to watch them. Cracker was
getting very tubby and we just
couldn't understand why!"

Then Lydia walked off and
I started sweeping again, but
when I looked up at Shine she was really staring
at me, like she was trying to tell me something.

I leaned on my broom and stared back at her.
"What is it, Shine?" I asked, and she just kept
looking at me. Then I realized – Lydia has given
me the perfect idea.

I'm going to set up a watch of my own, like
she did, but not from the office, obviously.
Shine's stable will make the perfect hiding place
and plus, she can keep me company – we'll be
a detective team! It won't be all night either, as
Jody checks on us at about quarter past 9 and
the activities don't finish till just after 8. I know
that if Courtney sneaks back out here it would
have to be between those times because she'd
be missed before or after. Shanice's brush was
definitely there when we went in for dinner,
after all, and wasn't there in the morning, so
that's the only time it could have been stolen.

I wanted to run and tell Beth and Millie about
my plan, but then I remembered how Millie
reacted before, so I've decided to do it alone

and only tell them after I've got the proof.

I've also been thinking about what's been taken so far and trying to work out what Courtney might go for next (if she comes out at all, that is). At first, I couldn't see the point of her taking those things.

I just didn't see why she would. I mean, if she actually used the ribbons, we'd all notice, and how would she explain suddenly having a new silk to her mum? She doesn't have her own pony so why would she need a body brush?

Then I realized – they're all things the girls were really proud of and that everyone said were nice. It's like she's taking things that get their owners lots of attention. Plus, they've all been taken from the tack room. Courtney

obviously doesn't want to risk stealing from the
bedrooms, where she might easily be caught.
So, I have a hunch she'll go for Aneela's stripey
lead rope next, because everyone's been saying
how nice it is and asking where she got it.

I hate sneaking around like this, but I really
need to get proof before I go to Jody. Okay,
I'm going out now. I'm taking my digital camera
with me to catch Courtney in the
act. Millie's busy in the kitchen
and I think Beth's with her, or
she might be on the phone in the
hall downstairs. Anyway, I'll have to go now
before they come back or it'll be too late.

7.20am on Thursday morning,
before the others have woken up

I'm sitting up in bed writing this.

Well, I wasn't expecting…

I still can't believe it…

Oh, I don't know where to start. Maybe I should just write everything down from where I left off.

Well, I sneaked out to the yard and I was in Shine's stable waiting with my camera. After a while, I heard someone coming right past Shine's door, so I had to duck down. As I bobbed back up again, I saw the tack room door swinging shut. I slipped out and hurried across to it, trying not to make a sound. Then I threw the door open, camera ready to catch Courtney in the act. She swung round, Aneela's stripey lead rope in her hand.

And that's when I got the shock of my life.

It wasn't Courtney, but Beth. As in my friend Beth.

She froze, staring at me, and the lead rope slithered to the floor.

"Beth! What are you doing with…" I began, but she just stared at me. "Oh, you had the same idea as me," I said then. "You were going to catch the thief too."

But Beth shook her head. Her shoulders slumped and she stared at the floor. "Sophie, I… I didn't mean to…" she mumbled.

I suddenly understood what she was saying and it made me shiver. I could hardly believe it. Could Beth really be the thief? "But Courtney…" I began.

"No," said Beth. "She didn't take the ribbons."

"So you *did* hear what I said to Millie!" I cried.

Beth nodded miserably. "Yes, but I didn't know what to say, so I pretended to be asleep. And yes, Courtney did put the ribbons back in Daisy's tack box, but I took them out again." Her voice cracked and she started to cry.

"But how could you take our things?" I demanded. "Especially Shanice's brush, when she saved up so hard and everything. And Daisy was really upset…"

Beth was sobbing by then and part of me wanted to go and give her a hug, but I also felt furious. "You're my friend," I said. "I can't believe you'd do something like this."

Beth sat down heavily on a pile of numnahs waiting for the wash. "I didn't really mean to," she gabbled. "It just sort of happened. I was in the

tack room on my own and I decided to try
Izzy's silk on my hat, just for a minute. So I took
it off hers but then I heard people coming and
I didn't know what to do, so I shoved it in my
pocket and hurried back on to the yard. I was
going to put it back later, but there wasn't a
good time. When she saw it was missing I didn't
know how to explain, so I sort of ended up
keeping it."

I sighed. "But what about Daisy's ribbons and
Shanice's brush? You can't say you didn't mean
to take those too."

Beth's shoulders slumped further. "I don't
know," she mumbled. "I just felt really sort of …
almost, like, jealous of them…"

"You mean, because they got attention for
having those nice things?" I suggested.

Beth thought for a moment then nodded
miserably and wiped her eyes on the sleeve of
her fleece. "Everyone else seems to get noticed

and not me," she sniffled. "Like with Dad, I feel invisible since he got this new girlfriend, Sarah. There's no time for me, I'm just in the way. It's obvious they'd rather do things on their own. And now he's asked her to move in with us and I don't, I don't…"

I was really surprised. "But you said everything was fine between you and your dad," I stuttered.

"It was … before Sarah came along. I had to pretend to Dad that everything was all right, but secretly I kept hoping that they'd split up and things would go back to being the way they were: just the two of us."

"Well, maybe they will," I said.

But Beth shook her head. "It's not going to happen. Just before I came here I found out she's moving in. I didn't say anything to you and Millie because I didn't want to even think about it during my holiday."

Then she dissolved into tears
again. This time I went and sat
down next to her. "Come
on, it's not as bad as
all that," I said stiffly.
"Why don't you
just tell your dad
how you feel?"

"I tried to," she
half-whispered, "but then I found myself saying
I was okay because I didn't want him to be
upset with me."

"I know how you feel," I admitted. "I was
happy with things as they were – just as me,
Mum and Dad. But then when they had Albie it
was like I didn't exist, apart from to do chores
and clean up after him. And they're always too
tired to do anything. But I can't tell them I wish
it was the three of us again – Mum would be
so upset."

Beth leaned against my shoulder then and I
didn't shrug her off. We both sat there quietly
for a while, thinking. I did feel sorry for her, but
I couldn't forget what she'd done. "Just because
you're having a hard time, that doesn't mean
you can steal things," I said, firmly.

"I know," she replied. "It's not an excuse. It
was wrong and I should never have done it. I'm
really not like that, honest." She started crying
again then, and said, "Please believe me."

"Look, I do believe you, but you have to talk
to your dad about how you feel," I told her. "But
first you have to put things right here."

"I'll put everything back the first chance I
get," she sniffled. "I promise. But…"
Beth looked up at me, and even
in the half light I could see that
she was nervous and scared.
"You won't tell on me, will you,
Sophie?" she almost whispered.

I thought about what might happen – a thief would probably be sent home in disgrace. Beth's dad would be furious. I didn't know what to do. I still don't. I mean, she's stolen things from my friends. I should tell, shouldn't I? But then, she was so upset, and I do believe she's sorry.

I didn't say yes or no, instead I just told her to go back in. She nodded, wiped her tears away and stumbled out of the tack room. I watched her dash round the side of the stables. When she'd gone, I slipped out too and turned to go the same way. But just then Lydia came out of the office. I couldn't run for the corner, it was too far. I just sort of froze as she walked up to me. "Sophie? What are you doing out here?" she asked.

"Erm, nothing," I said quickly.

She frowned at me in the dusky light, following my nervous glance to the tack room door, which was half open.

"I, er, I couldn't resist coming out to see
Shine, and I thought I'd just check the tack room
for, er..." I couldn't think of what
I possibly needed to check in the
tack room for. It was a fib and
Lydia knew it.

"Well, you shouldn't be out.
Off you go," she said.

I hurried back to the
farmhouse, heart pounding, and
I could feel her watching me as I turned the
corner by the stables, but I didn't dare look
back.

I went straight into the shower, then joined
everyone else downstairs for hot chocolate.

Luckily Beth had her shower after me, so
I managed to avoid her, and when she came
down for her hot chocolate I went upstairs,
saying how tired I was. So when my room-
mates came up I was already in bed, pretending

to be asleep. I didn't want Beth to ask me again
whether I was going to tell or not, because
I hadn't decided. I still haven't (while I was
thinking with my eyes shut I actually fell asleep
for real).

And I still don't know what to do about Beth.
I mean, how can we be friends now I know
what she's done? Surely I should only care about
Shanice and the other girls' feelings and not
Beth's? Yes, she's promised to put everything
back, and I really think she will, but is that
enough?

Right, I've decided I'm going to tell. Oh, but
what if Beth gets sent home in disgrace? That
would be awful, and her dad would be so angry
with her.

Oh wait, I think Beth's waking up. I'll go and
wash my face in the bathroom so we don't have
to talk.

Thursday morning, still

I'm writing this in the games room, while everyone's finishing their breakfast.

When I got back from the bathroom I couldn't avoid Beth any more. Millie went back downstairs to give Jody a hand with the breakfast, so it was just the two of us. I pretended to be busy folding my clothes, not looking at her.

"Sophie," she began, "I know you have to do what you think is right, but I've been so worried I've hardly slept. Are you going to talk to Jody about what I've done?"

I sighed and looked up. She was so upset, I knew I couldn't make it worse by telling. "Well, I really should … but no," I said.

Beth looked really relieved. "Thanks! Oh, thanks so much," she gabbled. "It was a mistake, I promise. It felt awful and I'll never do it again.

I'll put everything back today, the very first chance I get to slip out."

"Good," I said, then I grabbed my diary and made for the door. I didn't want to talk about it any more.

"Sophie," she said, and I paused in the doorway. "It's just, well, can we still be friends?" she asked shyly.

"Oh! Erm, I've got to go now," I mumbled, and hurried out without looking at her. I don't know if I want to be friends after this, I mean, how could I trust her?

It's time for yard duty now so I'm going to put this diary upstairs and forget all about what's happened. I'm so glad it's over. Beth'll put the stuff back and everything will be normal again and I can just carry on enjoying my holiday with my gorgeous pony.

It's after our lesson now, and I'm hiding in our room.

Everything's gone really wrong and it's hard to write – I'm still trembling from what just happened. I came up here to look for Beth but I can't find her anywhere, so I'm just going to lie on my bed and write this and calm down a bit. I feel like I never want to go downstairs again!

What happened was, after the lesson, Jody came up and asked me to untack Shine quickly and meet her in the kitchen. I'd had trouble with Shine again in Sally's lesson, and so she told me to get tougher, and I'd ended up getting all nervous and flustered. Jody didn't look happy and I thought she'd say I hadn't done well enough in Sally's group and I had to go back into Group A.

But it was worse than that. Much worse.

I got into the kitchen and Jody looked up from the papers on the table in front of her. "Ah, Sophie," she said. "Thanks for coming in. Look, this is a bit awkward but I have to ask – do you know anything about these things that have gone missing?"

I just stood there feeling completely confused. I couldn't think why she'd ask me especially, on my own. At first I thought she knew about Beth, but then I realized that there's no way she could. She said, "Sophie?" again and I realized I hadn't replied.

"I, er, I don't understand…" I began. Then it hit me – when Lydia saw me, she could have thought I was the thief!

She must have mentioned seeing me last night to Jody. Even though I hadn't actually done anything, I couldn't help blushing.

"I know I was out in the yard when I
shouldn't have been, but I'm not a thief!" I cried,
feeling panicky. "Please don't think that!"

I really wanted Jody to say, "Of course I don't
think that," but instead she just said, "So there's
nothing you want to tell me?"

There was a long silence. I kept my eyes
glued to the floor but I could feel her looking
at me. My mind was in a whirl of confusion – I
couldn't tell on Beth when I'd promised not to,
could I? Finally I shook my head. "No, nothing," I
mumbled.

"Sophie, I don't want to think badly of you,"
Jody said then. "But you were seen on the yard
when you shouldn't have been and the tack
room door was open. I'm not saying you took
those things, but I can't help feeling you're hiding
something."

Just then, there was a sound from outside
in the hall. Aneela poked her head round the

doorway. Jody put on a forced smile and said,
"Could we just have a moment, please?"
Aneela gave me a funny look
and I hurriedly stared at the
floor again.

Jody sighed, and said,
"Well, if you're not going to
tell me anything, you'd better
go." I couldn't stand the
disappointment in her voice.
It's awful that she thinks I could
have stolen those things. And
even worse that she might
ring my parents.

My first thought was to find
Beth, and tell her things had changed
and that she had to own up or I'd get the
blame. But when I got to the games room, Millie
and Beth weren't there. The other girls were
all whispering together and when they saw me

77

they suddenly stopped. Aneela glared at me
and put her arm round Shanice. She must have
overheard me and Jody in the kitchen, and told
everyone what happened. Now they all think
I'm the thief! My heart was pounding and
I couldn't even bear to look at Shanice.
I just turned and ran out.

I tried to find Beth in the yard, but she
wasn't with Millie, who was helping Johnny in
the office. She wasn't in the barn with Monsoon,
either. I raced back indoors and came upstairs,
but she's not here.

Oh, she's…

It's still Thursday,
but after lunch

I've found a little space round the side of the
barn so I can be on my own.

I suddenly had to stop writing earlier because
Beth came into our room.

"When Aneela said you... Well, I panicked,"
she told me, shakily. "I ran up to the top field –
I was really scared and I didn't know what to
do." She took a deep breath then and said, "But
I do now. I've come to get the things I took, and
I'm going downstairs right now, to tell everyone
the truth. Don't worry, they won't think it was
you for long."

She leaned over her bed and rummaged in
the bottom corner, under the covers. She pulled
out Shanice's brush, and the purple silk and the
ribbons. She was very pale and her hands were
trembling.

"But what if you get sent home?" I asked. "Won't your dad be really angry?"

Beth's eyes filled with tears but she looked determined. "I'll just have to face that," she said. "You've been such a good friend to me, Sophie, I'm not going to let you down again. I'd better…" And she gestured to the door.

I suddenly found myself standing up. "I'll come with you," I said.

She smiled a watery smile. "Thanks."

So we went down to the games room together, Beth clutching the stolen things. The other girls were all chatting and Jody was there too, clearing the cups and snacks away.

"Jody, I've got something to tell you," Beth began, and then burst into tears.

I put my arm round her as she held out the
missing things.

Beth didn't need to say anything else. Jody
understood straight away. "Oh, Beth," she said,
"you have been a silly girl, haven't you?" The
other girls gradually fell silent and gathered
around us.

"I'm so sorry," Beth said to Izzy, then Daisy,
then Shanice as she handed back their things,
but none of them said, "That's okay."

For a moment there was an awful silence.
Then Izzy mumbled, "She should go home."

We all looked at Jody. She sighed. I could see
she was really disappointed in Beth. I was certain
she was going to send her home. But then Jody
said, "As it's Friday tomorrow and Beth has
owned up, she'll be staying to the end of the
week. However, I will be speaking privately to
her father tomorrow, and she'll be excluded
from the hack this afternoon as punishment.

Beth, you can do poo-picking in the field instead.
Now, why don't you pop upstairs and wash
your face?" With that, Beth raced out of the
room without looking at anyone.

"Now, come on, time for you all to get back
on the yard, there's a lot to do," Jody told us.

As I was turning to go, Aneela caught my arm
and said, "Sorry for thinking you were the thief,
Sophie."

I was going to be cross with her, but then
I remembered how I'd done that too, over
Courtney and the silk, and I blushed. "That's
okay," I told her. I knew how bad she felt
because I felt like that too. I should never have
jumped to conclusions.

I'm glad no one thinks I'm a thief any more.
I just want things to go back to normal, but I
don't know if I can be friends with Beth again.

Thursday night,
in bed after lights out

We didn't have a lecture this afternoon, just an extra-long hack in the countryside. Beth didn't come as she was poo-picking the upper field, and some of the other girls were saying mean things about her as we rode along, but I didn't want to join in. I thought Beth had been very brave to own up. Millie didn't seem interested in being nasty about Beth either, and instead we just concentrated on having fun. Shine was so brilliant, she really loved being out in the countryside! When we were going through the woods, a bird flew out of the bushes and Shine did her spooky thing of going sideways again. I didn't mind, though, and I just steered her back on to the path without even worrying. I realized that

83

I just need to do that in the manège, as if it's nothing, and then Shine will behave and I won't get panicky. I'm definitely going to put that into practice tomorrow.

We had a canter across a stubble field too and it was fantastic. Millie stopped holding Tally back and he galloped the whole way – and Shine followed! It was brilliant, just hearing the pounding of their hooves and leaving everyone else behind, even the older girls! Shine got so excited I had to do a circle at the other end of the field to slow her down before she'd go back into trot, and again I just calmly did it and she got the message. When we finally halted, me and Millie just looked at each other, grinning and catching our breath. In fact, even thinking about it is making me smile now. I did miss Beth a bit, though. It seemed strange just being Millie and me.

When we got back and went in for tea, Beth was already in the kitchen, helping Jody to serve up. We were all talking about the hack and how much fun we'd had. But no one really included Beth, and when she did try to say something to Izzy and Aneela they just ignored her. Millie and I weren't exactly talking to her either, but I didn't like seeing her so left out. I was really embarrassed when Jody leaned over the table and said, "Come on, girls, everyone makes mistakes, and it took a lot of courage for Beth to own up. So let's put this behind us, shall we? We're here to enjoy our ponies and the riding, remember?"

There was a really awkward silence that went

on for ages and ages after that, but people do
seem to be being a bit nicer to Beth now.

After tea, Courtney did my make-up and she
let me practise my tail plaiting on her hair. After
a couple of goes I started getting the hang of
it, so I'm definitely going to try it out on Shine
tomorrow.

This evening we watched a DVD
of famous three-day eventers at
Burghley Horse Trials. Jody made us
popcorn, and we were glued to the
TV, all going "Wow!" and "Eeek!"
together as the eventers cleared these massive
jumps. It was good because Beth could easily join
in and no one was not speaking to anyone.

I can't believe it's my last day here tomorrow
– and my last ride on Shine! I can't wait for the
gymkhana! I'm going to give Dad my camera
to take loads of pix – and hopefully I'll win a
rosette too!

Friday, lunchtime

I'm quickly writing this before our parents arrive and the gymkhana starts!

It's really funny because everyone keeps crashing about up here, looking for their hair bobbles and changing their mind about what top to wear and stuff. I got changed really quickly into my smart clothes – I'd planned what I was going to wear for the gymkhana about 3 days before I even got here, I was looking forward to it so much!

We had great fun on the yard just now – we tied all our ponies up next to each other so we could get them ready for this afternoon. We shared the box of ribbons and the quarter-mark stencils and everything, and borrowed things from each other. It was like a pampering party for ponies.

Here are all the things I did to spruce up Shine for the gymkhana:

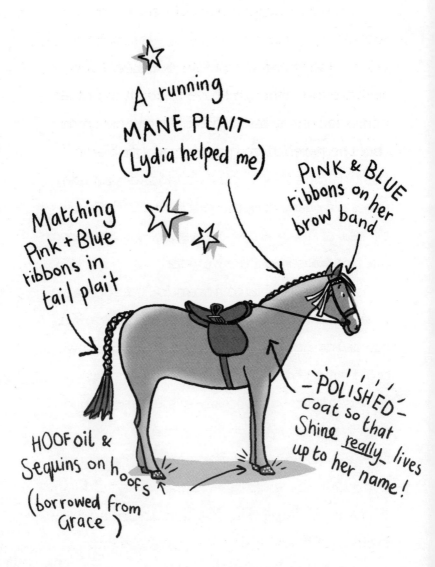

Then we all cleaned our tack until it was spotless and gleaming. Hopefully me and Shine will win the tack and turnout competition after all that effort, although I have to admit the other ponies looked fantastic too. Courtney did some cool chequer-pattern quarter marks on Flame, and Daisy did the tail plait with ribbons in it that Lydia showed us on Tuesday. When she got a bit stuck halfway, Beth offered to help and Daisy said yes please, so that was good.

When Beth came back over to Monsoon, I gave her a secret grin and she grinned back. Yes, I've decided to be friends with her again. Then Shine stretched her neck and nuzzled Beth's shoulder, like she was pleased that things were turning out okay too.

In our last lesson this morning we had a go at neck reining, which Sally explained is this way of putting both reins in one hand and using the pressure of them against the pony's neck to steer. She said it makes riding much easier when you're holding things for the gymkhana games, but when we tried it, we all kept going the wrong way and nearly crashing into each other. Sally laughed and said, "On second thoughts, maybe just use both hands on the reins or it's going to be chaos this afternoon!"

We had a go at some of the games we'll be playing too, so that everyone knew what to do. Shine's quite quick at the bending, and all the stuff I've remembered this week about how to use my legs as a pair to keep her straight really helped. I stayed relaxed with her too, and when she tried to skitter about I just kept going as if it didn't bother me. She soon settled down and Sally even noticed and said well done, so that was fab! Let's hope me and Shine win a rosette this afternoon – I've never won anything before and I'd love to have one to stick on my wall!

Friday, dinner time.
At home again!

I've only just got home and I haven't even unpacked, but I'm writing this straight away so I don't forget anything.

When my family got here, I was surprised at how pleased I was to see them. Yes, even Albie! All the other girls loved him, and it was really cool when they wanted him to grip their fingers and asked me loads of questions about him. I showed Mum, Dad and Albie round the yard and introduced them to Shine. She was in her stable, all tacked up and ready to go, and Mum and Dad made a big fuss of her. They were really proud when I told them I got moved up a group.

When everyone's parents had arrived it was time for the gymkhana. I had butterflies in my stomach but I couldn't stop smiling. The first thing we did was lead our ponies out of the stables and into the manège for the tack and turnout competition. We had to stand next to them, very straight and tall, and try not to laugh when Johnny and Lydia came round to judge. That was quite hard because Lydia looked under Shine's tail to make sure I'd cleaned her bottom properly (which I had – yucky but important!). And when they were inspecting Cracker, he did a wee and Lydia said, "Well, that's not very gentlemanly, is it?" and we all burst out giggling.

Of course, I had my fingers crossed for me and Shine, but I was really pleased for Daisy when she won. We all gave her a clap and she took a big bow, and then it was time to mount up for the games.

♡ Sophie and Shine ♡

What happened was, the Group A people went against each other while we cheered them on and then we had our go while they cheered for us. These are some of the races we did:

Walk, trot, canter – You go up the manège in walk, back in trot, and up again in canter. It was so funny in our heat because Tally didn't understand the concept of trying to go slowly, and he kept breaking into trot during the walking part, so he and Millie got sent back to the beginning three times.

Stepping Stones – We had to canter up, then get off and step from straw bale to staw bale while leading our ponies. That was such a fun game!

Ball and racket – We had to balance a ball on a tennis racket and ride steadily enough to keep it there all the way across the manège. Izzy and Millie had no chance with their boisterous ponies tearing off in canter, but I was doing really well.

Then Shine spooked at Millie's flying ball and skittered sideways – oh, well! Aneela ended up winning on Charm, who's about the best behaved pony you can possibly get. Shanice won the Group A comp on Prince, and I was so happy for her and clapped extra hard when she got her rosette.

Bending – Guess what? I actually won this one! Shine was wonderful and really listened to my legs.

I was so proud when I got my rosette for the bending, and everyone clapped (and Dad took loads of pix!). It felt amazing! And then I was even more amazed to get an extra-special prize. Jody said, "We've decided to give a special award to someone who has shown the most improvement this week. So much, in fact, that she moved up a group. Sophie!"

Everyone clapped again, and when I looked over at Mum and Dad they were beaming the biggest smiles you could imagine.

When we came off the yard, I looked for

Beth and realized that while everyone was chatting to their families, she was leading Monsoon to the barn with Lydia. That's when I realized Jody was probably having a private word with her dad. I felt really sorry for Beth, but it was nice of Jody to wait till after the gymkhana, in case he was really angry.

I gave Shine a good brush down and took out her plaits, then got her some more fresh water even though she didn't really need any. I was just trying to delay saying goodbye for as long as possible! But in the end, I heard Mum calling me so I put my brushes away and flung my arms round her neck. "Oh, Shine, thanks for being my wonderful pony for the week," I said. "Even if I can't come back next year, and even if I'm ever lucky enough to get my own pony, I'll never forget you."

Shine whinnied and tossed her head, so I think that, somehow, she understood.

Just as I was bolting the stable door, Beth came over to me. "Dad wasn't furious after all," she said. "Just really worried about me."

I said, "That's good, but you will still tell him how you feel about things, won't you?"

Beth nodded, and we had a big goodbye hug. She's going to write to me and tell me what happens when they have the talk about his girlfriend moving in. Of course, nothing's ever perfect, but I think everything will work out okay for her.

I think things are going to work out okay for me too, actually. When we'd all said goodbye and I'd taken loads of pix and checked I'd got everything (and had a bit of a cry saying goodbye to Shine!) we finally got me and my stuff and Albie loaded into the car.

After we'd waved and waved to everyone and turned out into the road, Mum said, "I'm glad you had such a great time, but we really did miss you, Sophie. I don't know how I've coped without you this week. You're so helpful with the baby, I really do appreciate it. I'll take you riding more often from now on. We won't let all this improvement go to waste, I promise."

"Thanks, Mum," I said. "And I don't mind helping with Albie. He's okay, I suppose." I was amazed to hear myself say that, but I really meant it. It's taken a week away from my baby bro to make me realize I'm glad we've got him after all (even if he does cry a lot!). I don't feel like I want it to just be the three of us any more. "In fact, I think we should make our family even bigger," I said then.

"Oh, no way, I'm not having another one!" cried Mum.

"I wasn't talking about a baby," I giggled. "I'm thinking of a pony!"

Mum laughed then and Dad said, "We'll have to see about that. Perhaps if you keep on improving as much as you have we could think about looking for a share. Maybe."

Wow! I couldn't believe he said they'd half-think about it – even for one second! I squealed so loudly it made Albie laugh. I know I'll have to prove I really deserve a pony, and show them how dedicated I am to my riding, but at least he didn't say absolutely no way!

I'm going to print out my pix now, well, after I've taken my dirty clothes downstairs and helped get Albie ready for bed. See, I've started being the perfect daughter already – that ought to help persuade them on the pony front!

Tomorrow I'm planning to make a collage of my pictures from Sunnyside and put my rosettes on it too! And in the middle there'll be a big picture of me with Shine, my wonderful pony for the week!

PONY CAMP
diaries

Learn all about
the world of ponies!

Glossary

Bending – directing the horse to ride correctly around a curve.

Bit – the piece of metal that goes inside the horse's mouth. Part of the bridle.

Chase Me Charlie – a show jumping game where the jumps get higher and higher.

Currycomb – a comb with rows of metal teeth used to clean (to curry) a pony's coat.

Dandy brush – a brush with hard bristles that removes the dirt, hair, and any other debris stirred up by the currycomb.

Frog – the triangular soft part on the underside of the horse's hoof. It's very important to clean around it with a hoof pick.

Girth – the band attached to the saddle and buckled around the horse's barrel to keep the saddle in place.

Grooming – the daily cleaning and caring for the horse to keep them healthy and make them beautiful for competitions. A full groom includes brushing your horse's coat, mane and tail and picking out the hooves.

Gymkhana – a fun event full of races and other competitions.

Hands – a way to measure the height of a horse.

Glossary

Mane – the long hair on the back of a horse's neck. Perfect for plaiting!

Manège – an enclosed training area for horses and their riders.

Numnah – a piece of material that lies under the saddle and stops it from rubbing against the horse's back.

Paces – a horse has four main paces, each made up of an evenly repeated sequence of steps. From slowest to quickest, these are the walk, trot, canter and gallop.

Plodder – a slow, reliable horse.

Pommel – the raised part at the front of the saddle.

Pony – a horse under 14.2 hands in height.

Rosette – a rose-shaped decoration with ribbons awarded as a prize! Usually, a certain colour matches the place you come in during the competition.

Stirrups – foot supports attached to the sides of a horse's saddle.

Tack – the main pieces of the horse's equipment, including the saddle and bridle. Tacking up a horse means getting them ready for riding.

✑ Pony Colours ✑

*Ponies come in all kinds of **colours**. These are some of the most common!*

Bay – Bay ponies have rich brown bodies and black manes, tails and legs.

Black – A true black pony will have no brown hairs and the black can be so pure that it looks a bit blue!

Chestnut – Chestnut ponies have reddish-brown coats that vary from light to dark red with no black points.

Dun – A dun pony has a sandy-coloured body, with a black mane, tail and legs.

Grey – Grey ponies come in a range of colour varieties, including dapple grey, steel grey, and rose grey.

Palomino – Palominos have a sandy-coloured body with a white or cream mane and tail. Their coats can range from pale yellow to bright gold!

Piebald – Piebald ponies have a mixture of black patches and white patches – like a cow!

Skewbald – Skewbald ponies have patches of white and brown.

~ Pony Markings ~

*As well as the main body colour, many ponies also have white **markings** on their faces and legs!*

On the legs:

Socks – run up above the fetlock but lower than the knee. The fetlock is the joint above the hoof.

Stockings – extend to at least the bottom of the horse's knee, sometimes higher.

On the face:

Blaze – a wide, straight stripe down the face from in between the eyes to the muzzle.

Snip – a white marking on the horse's muzzle, between the nostrils.

Star – a white marking between the eyes.

Stripe – the same as a blaze but narrower.

White/bald face – a very wide blaze that goes out past the eyes, making most of the horse's face look white!

Fan-tack-stic Cleaning Tips!

*Get your **tack** shining in no time with these top tips!*

- Clean your tack after every use, if you can. Otherwise, make sure you at least rinse the bit under running water and wash off any mud or sweat from your girth after each ride.
- The main things you will need are:
  - bars of saddle soap
  - a soft cloth
  - a sponge
  - a bottle of leather conditioner
- As you clean your bit, check that it has no sharp edges and isn't too worn.
- Use a bridle hook or saddle horse to hold your bridle and saddle as you clean them. If you don't have a saddle horse, you can hang a blanket over a gate to put the saddle on. Avoid hanging your bridle on a single hook or nail because the leather might crack!

- Make sure you look carefully at the bridle before undoing it so that you know how to put it back together!
- Use the conditioner to polish the leather of the bridle and saddle and make them sparkle!
- Check under your numnah before you clean it. If the dirt isn't evenly spread on both sides, you might not be sitting evenly as you ride.
- Polish your metalwork occasionally. Cover the leather parts around it with a cloth and only polish the rings – not the mouthpiece, because that would taste horrible!

∾ Saddle Up! ∾

Find out how much you know about riding equipment with this fun quiz!

1. You should keep your saddle in great condition by:

   a. Cleaning it regularly with saddle soap
   b. Rinsing it down with hot water after every use
   c. Only using it on Sundays

2. The girth is:

   a. A strap that goes around the pony's neck
   b. A strap that secures the saddle to the pony's back
   c. A cool belt to jazz up your jodhpurs

3. When jumping, riders often:

   a. Shorten their stirrups a little
   b. Lengthen their stirrups a little
   c. Cross their stirrups over the front of the saddle

4. The following is NOT a type of bit:

   a. An eggbutt, double-jointed snaffle bit
   b. A Pelham bit with a rubber mullen mouthpiece
   c. A Sanderson super-snazzy bit

5. The following is NOT part of a bridle:

a. The stirrup leathers
b. The cheek pieces
c. The brow band

6. Under the pony's saddle, you should place at least one:

a. Turn-out rug
b. Saddle pad
c. Sandwich for when you get hungry on your ride

7. The following is not part of a saddle:

a. The skirt
b. The pommel
c. The dress

8. After every ride, you should always remember to:

a. Rinse your bit
b. Clean your whole bridle
c. Brush your hair

Pretty Plaits!

Follow this step-by-step guide to give your pony a perfect tail plait!

1. Start at the very top of the tail and take two thin bunches of hair from either side, plaiting them into a strand in the centre.

2. Continue to pull in bunches from either side and plait down the centre of the tail.

3. Keep plaiting like this, making sure you're pulling the hair tightly to keep the plait from unravelling!

4. When you reach the end of the dock – where the bone ends – stop taking in bunches from the side but keep plaiting downwards until you run out of hair.

5. Fasten with a plait band!

Gymkhana Ready!

Get your pony looking spectacular for the gymkhana with these grooming ideas!

A running MANE PLAIT

Ribbons on her brow band

Matching ribbons in tail plait

POLISHED Coat

HOOF oil & Sequins on hooves

Turn the page for a sneak peek
at another story in the series!

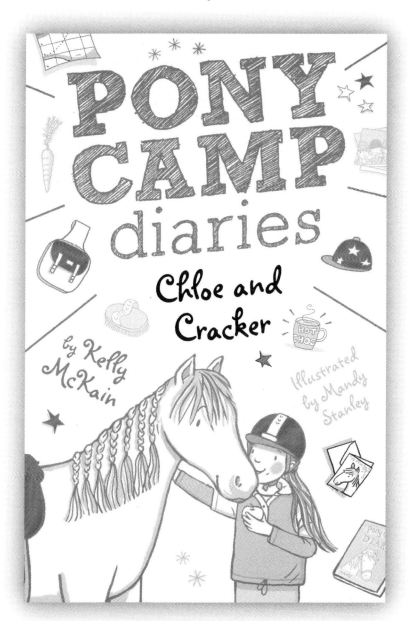

PONY
CAMP
diaries

Chloe and
Cracker

by Kelly
McKain

Illustrated
by Mandy
Stanley

Monday morning
– at Pony Camp!

Jody, the lady who runs Sunnyside Stables, gave
me this cool diary when I arrived just now. Her
letter at the front says it's to write down all the
adventures I have this week. It's fantastic here
– there are two outdoor manèges and lots of
cute ponies and dogs everywhere and even
a swimming pool! I'm hoping to have lots of
adventures – especially jumping ones!

I really wanted to come on this week because
when Mum rang up and spoke to Jody, she said
they're holding a special jumping competition on
the last day. In our lessons, we're going to work
on building up to an eight-jump course, and it's
even going to include some cross-country fences
for fun – I can't wait!

I love jumping but I've only done a couple
of smaller courses at clear round events at my

local riding school. I'm really hoping to improve while I'm here – and I'm desperate to go clear in Friday's competition.

The reasons I want a clear round so much are:

a. because I've never had one before so it will be a big challenge for me and

b. to make Dad proud of me.

Although Dad knows how much I love ponies (I'm always talking about getting my own one day!), he's never actually seen me ride. He's always working, even at weekends. But he said he'll really, really try to come with Mum to pick me up on Friday, then he'll be able to see me in the jumping competition and I can amaze him with my clear round (fingers crossed!). I really hope he keeps his word and doesn't get stuck at work as usual.

Jody

Sally

As soon as I got here, I kept asking Jody what we'll be doing every day because I was really excited. She smiled and said Sally, the instructor, will explain that when everyone arrives, but I really, really wanted to know straight away so she gave me a copy of the timetable to stick into my diary. She has warned me that it will change, though, because we have special activities on some days. Like, it says in her letter we're going on a treasure hunt this week – that sounds really fun!

Here's the timetable for the week:

Pony Camp Timetable

8am: Wake up, get dressed, have breakfast

8.45am: Help on the yard, bring in the ponies from field, muck out stables, do feeds, etc.

9.30am: Prepare ponies for morning lessons (quick groom, tack up, etc.)

10am: Morning riding lesson

11am: Morning break - drink and biscuits

11.20am: Pony Care lecture

12.30pm: Lunch and free time

2pm: Afternoon riding lesson

3pm: Break - drink and biscuits

3.20pm: Pony Care lecture

4.30pm: Jobs around the yard (i.e. cleaning tack, sweeping up, mixing evening feeds, turning out ponies)

5.30pm: Free time before dinner

6pm: Dinner (and clearing up!)

7pm: Evening activity

8.30pm: Showers and hot chocolate

9.30pm: Lights out and NO TALKING!

Wow! There's so much to do here! I just can't wait to find out which pony I'm getting – having my own pony to look after for a whole week will be fab!

This morning we're having an assessment lesson where we all ride in together, and then Sally will decide who goes in which group. So the timetable's different already because there's no lecture this morning. It's now 10.35am and not everyone is here yet, including the girls who are sharing my room – but, oh, now I can hear talking and clumping on the stairs. Maybe it's them!

Two minutes later

It *was* them!

The two girls I'm sharing with have gone downstairs to help on the yard – we are all still waiting for a couple of others to arrive, but the adults keep telling each other that there's a hold-up on the M3 so we're running a bit later than planned.

I'm going down in a minute but first I just wanted to do a quick profile of my room-mates for my diary.

Name: Isabella

Age: 12

Lives: Buckinghamshire, which is sort of near to London but still in the countryside.

Description: Quite tall for 12, goes to a school for

girls only, has amazing green eyes and long wavy brown hair and plays the cello and has packed three different swimsuits because she couldn't decide which to bring (I've only got one!). She says her friends call her Bella, and we can too (how cool!).

Name: Georgia

Age: 12

Lives: Georgia comes all the way from Devon, which I suppose isn't actually far from here, but it's a long way from where I live (i.e. London).

Description: Short blondish hair. She seems very sensible and mature for 12, but she's also really friendly so that's okay. She has two younger brothers and one younger sister and says she has to help her mum and dad look after them quite a lot.

The best thing is that Isabella and Georgia are both really into jumping too and they also chose this week specially to come to Sunnyside, so they could spend lots of time focusing on it. Also, they're both really nice and are not leaving me out just because I'm a weeny bit younger than them, which older girls can sometimes do.

Oh, I have to go – Bella's calling me down to the yard. Maybe it's time to find out which ponies we're getting. I'm so excited just thinking about it! Fingers crossed mine's a good jumper!

Still Monday morning,
in our break

I am quickly writing this because I've got something exciting to put down that can't wait till later. The girls who were delayed are here now and we're just about to have our assessment lesson. But even though we haven't been given our ponies yet I have already met the perfect one for me.

What happened was, when I got outside, Jody explained that while we were waiting for the last two girls to arrive, we could get on with some yard work. She gave me mucking-out duty with this really nice stable girl called Lydia. That's when I met Charm, who is an amazingly gorgeous grey Connemara. I fell

in love with him straight away and Lydia said I
could lead him out and tie him up in the yard
while we did his stable. I gave him a big stroke
and pat on the way and he whinnied and
nuzzled into my T-shirt.

Lydia

While we were working I asked
Lydia about him and she told me
what a great jumper he is. That
just made me want him to be my
pony even more!

When Lydia and I had put the
new straw down on top of the
clean bits of bedding and spread it
all out, I got to lead Charm back in,
and I whispered to him that I really
hoped he'd be my pony for the
week. After a while, the other girls
arrived and Jody called us all back into the main
yard and introduced us to each other and the
Sunnyside Stables team.

As well as me and Bella and Georgia there is Millie, Jody's daughter, who I read about in the welcome letter. The girls sharing her room are called Suki and Mai and they go to an international school in London. They are both eight and three-quarters and are actually from Japan.

Suki   Mai

Then there are the little ones, Olivia, Asha and Joelle (who is only just seven and the youngest of all), and they're in a room together.

Olivia   Asha   Joelle

Me, Bella and Georgia are all really excited about the jumping and we're crossing our fingers that we get put in the group to do it. Bella and Georgia have jumped a bit but neither of them have done a competition yet, so I've probably got the most experience, even though it's not much.

I really, really hope I've got Charm. I've worked out I've got a 33.3333333333% chance of getting him – he's a bit big for the younger girls and Millie has her own pony, of course, and so I reckon it will be between me, Georgia and Bella.

Also available...

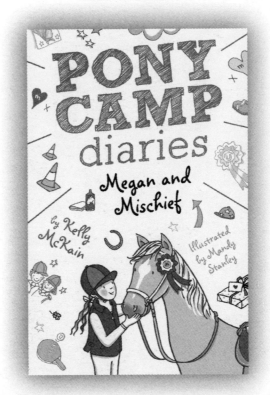

Megan and Mischief

I'm so excited to be here at Pony Camp!

I can't wait to meet my pony, but I'm a little
nervous too, because I've asked for a really fast
one. I'm ready to be Megan the Brave - hopefully
I can rise to the challenge!

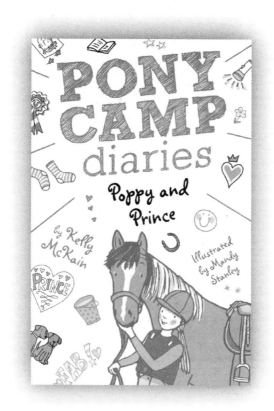

Poppy and Prince

I can't believe I'm finally here at Pony Camp!

The only thing is, I haven't ridden a pony since my big fall at a show jumping competition last month. I hope I can control my nerves and get back in the saddle!

Kelly McKain

Kelly McKain is a best-selling children's and YA author with more than 40 books published in more than 20 languages. She lives in the beautiful Surrey Heath area with her family and loves horses, dancing, yoga, singing, walking, and being in nature. She came up with the idea for the Pony Camp Diaries while she was helping young riders at a summer camp, just like the one at Sunnyside Stables! She enjoys hanging out at the Holistic Horse and Pony Centre, where she plays with and rides cute Smartie and practices her natural horsemanship skills with the Quantum Savvy group. Her dream is to do some bareback, bridleless jumping like New Zealand Free Riding ace Alycia Burton, but she has a ways to go yet!